CONTENTS

MEET BUG TEAM ALPHA

Bug Team Alpha is the most elite Special Operations force of the Colonial Armed Forces of the Earth Colonial Coalition. Each member has an insect's DNA surgically grafted onto his or her human DNA. With special abilities and buglike features, these soldiers are trained to tackle the most dangerous and unique combat missions. Their home base is *Space Station Prime*.

Ariel "Dragonfly" Carter

A human female with dragonfly wings grafted onto her shoulder blades. She is slender and lightweight, always on her tiptoes and ready for flight.

Rank. Commander
Age. 30 Earth Standard Years
Place of Origin. Earth,
  European Hemisphere
Hair. Blonde
Eyes. Blue
Height. 1.8 metres (5 feet, 11 inches)

Akiko "Radar" Murasaki

A human female with cranial antennae grafted onto her forehead. The antennae sense vibrations and can determine the length between and shape of objects in dark spaces.

Rank. Lieutenant
Age. 28 Earth Standard Years
Place of Origin. Earth,
  Asian Hemisphere
Hair. Brown
Eyes. Brown
Height. 1.58 metres (5 feet, 2 inches)

Anushka "Spoor" Kumar

A human female with combination DNA from several scenting insects. Nasal cavity folds open to expose scenting filaments that can detect even the smallest percentage of compounds in the air.

Rank. Lieutenant
Age. 28 Earth Standard Years
Place of Origin. Earth Colony Amaranth
Hair. Brown
Eyes. Brown
Height. 1.65 metres (6 feet, 5 inches)

Madhuri "Scorpion" Singh

A human female with spikes grafted onto her body. She can knock out an enemy with her venom.

Rank. Lieutenant
Age. 24 Earth Standard Years
Place of Origin. Earth Colony Shiva Three
Hair. Brown
Eyes. Brown
Height. 1.80 metres (5 feet, 11 inches)

Gustav "Burrow" Von Braun

A human male with digger beetle arms grafted onto his torso. He is heavyset and very strong and muscular.

Rank. Lieutenant
Age. 24 Earth Standard Years
Place of Origin. Earth, European Hemisphere
Hair. Brown
Eyes. Brown
Height. 1.68 metres (5 feet, 6 inches)

Liu "Hopper" Yu

A human male with grasshopper legs grafted onto his hips. Footpads take the place of footwear. He is slender and always springy, ready to jump.

Rank. Lieutenant
Age. 21 Earth Standard Years
Place of Origin. Earth, Asian Hemisphere
Hair: None, head is shaved
Eyes. Brown
Height. 1.88 metres (6 feet, 2 inches)

CHAPTER 1

General Barrett stood in his office on *Space Station Prime*. The megastructure orbited above planet Earth. The planet was a beautiful big blue marble with bright white clouds, vibrant green vegetation, tall mountains and vast deserts.

General Barrett looked at the planet through the viewport window. The sight normally made him feel calm and peaceful. But the general was not feeling calm or peaceful right now. He ran a hand over his bald scalp and turned his back to the view as he listened to the report coming in over the audio comm from the

Special Ops team, Bug Team Alpha. The dossiers of the operatives involved were displayed on a screen in front of him:

— — — — — — — — —

Commander Ariel "Dragonfly" Carter. Dragonfly wing DNA graft. Flight. Age: 30 Earth Standard Years. Planet of origin: Earth, European Hemisphere.

— — — — — — — — —

Lt Akiko "Radar" Murasaki. Cranial antennae DNA graft. Vibration detection. Age: 28 Earth Standard Years. Planet of origin: Earth, Asian Hemisphere.

— — — — — — — — —

Lt Gustav "Burrow" Von Braun. Digger beetle arm and leg flange DNA graft. Enhanced tunnelling abilities and strength. Age: 24 Earth Standard Years. Planet of origin: Earth, European Hemisphere.

— — — — — — — — —

Lt Liu "Hopper" Yu. Grasshopper DNA graft. Leaping ability. Age: 21 Earth Standard Years. Planet of origin: Earth, Asian Hemisphere.

— — — — — — — — —

Lt Anushka "Spoor" Kumar. Experimental combination DNA graft from several scenting insects.

A ridge on the nasal cavity folds open to expose scenting filaments. Age: 28 Earth Standard Years. Planet of origin: Earth Colony Amaranth.

— — — — — — — — —

Lt Madhuri "Scorpion" Singh. Scorpion DNA graft. Scorpion spikes on wrists; scorpion venom modified to knock out enemy, not poison. Age: 24 Earth Standard Years. Planet of origin: Earth Colony Shiva Three.

— — — — — — — — —

"It was an ambush, sir," Lt Anushka "Spoor" Kumar informed her superior officer.

General Barrett was the highest-ranking military officer in the Colonial Armed Forces. Bug Team Alpha was the most elite Special Operations team. They answered only to General Barrett or to the president of the Earth Colonial Coalition.

Not only were the Bug Team members trained for unique and unusual missions, their bodies were also specially designed for it. Each member of Bug Team Alpha had a different insect's DNA surgically grafted onto his or her human DNA. It gave them special powers. It also gave each of them specific insectlike appearances and abilities.

Bug Team Alpha was usually assigned to the most difficult and dangerous missions. This one had been a little . . . different.

"An ambush? At a wedding?" Barrett replied in astonishment.

The general's tall, lean body straightened in surprise.

"Yes, sir. It was a good thing the Bug Team was there," Spoor said.

"You were there as representatives of the Earth Colonial Coalition to the Imperial Government of the planet Zohatepa. You were supposed to be diplomatic guests, not a combat team," Barrett mentioned as he paced his office irritably.

"Sorry, sir. It didn't work out that way, sir," Spoor apologized. "A rival clan tried to take out the entire Imperial Family while they were gathered at the wedding. Their coup attempt failed."

"What's the status of Commander Dragonfly?" Barrett asked. "Why is a lieutenant giving me this report instead of the team leader?"

"She was wounded, sir. Blaster fire came at her from behind. It . . . it burned her wings pretty badly, sir,"

Spoor reported. Her voice lost its crispness and shook with emotion. "She's in the Imperial Infirmary right now."

"And what's the status of the rest of you?" the general asked firmly.

"No other injuries to report, sir," Spoor replied, recovering her composure.

"Very good," Barrett let himself sigh in relief. Despite his gruff military exterior, the members of Bug Team Alpha held a special place with him. "I want a full report in 11 Earth Standard Hours."

"Yes, sir," Spoor responded crisply.

"And get back to *Space Station Prime* as soon as possible," the general ordered.

General Barrett ended the transmission. Then he turned back to look at the big blue marble that was Earth, trying to feel calm and peaceful.

After five Earth Standard Days, the Bug Team boarded their long-range transport ship and left planet

Zohatepa. They were given a parade and an Imperial escort to the spaceport in gratitude for their actions against the coup.

Commander Ariel "Dragonfly" Carter hardly noticed any of it. She was on a medical stretcher and sedated. The rest of her team wished they had the same excuse. They were not comfortable with this sort of attention. They were a Special Operations team, not celebrities.

The Bug Team relaxed once their transport ship was flying through hyperspace and heading back towards Earth. Their transport ship was a Coalition diplomatic yacht with several sleeping cabins, a galley and a common eating and lounging area.

It was more than the Bug Team was used to. They usually travelled in stealth ships with tight quarters. But the mission to Zohatepa needed a vessel worthy of a Coalition diplomatic party, and so the Bug Team got to travel in style.

"I just checked on the commander in her room. She's asleep," Lt Akiko "Radar" Murasaki informed her teammates as she walked into the lounging area where they were gathered. It was one of the rare times they were all dressed in civilian clothing and not combat gear.

"That's good," Lt Gustav "Burrow" Von Braun said. "The more she rests, the faster she'll recover."

"Thanks for your prognosis, 'Doctor' Burrow," Lt Liu "Hopper" Yu teased good-naturedly as he bounced out of the galley on his long grasshopper legs. He carried a platter piled high with freshly cooked food. Lt Madhuri "Scorpion" Singh followed him with a tray full of drinks hooked over the spikes that provided her with her code name.

"That smells good!" Lt Spoor commented as she came into the lounge from the bridge. She had finished setting the ship's course on autopilot and was free to step away from the controls. Spoor opened her nasal flaps to breathe in the delicious aromas.

"I never have time to cook anymore," Hopper replied. "And travelling on a ship with a galley is a treat."

He set the platter on the central dining table and the Bug Team crowded around it eagerly. There was Terran rice and Andorian blue potatoes smothered in curry sauce, roasted giant mushrooms from Pandoros, handmade biscuits and sweet, stewed fruit for dessert.

"You did all of this from the ship's freeze-dried packets?" Burrow exclaimed as he tried one, then two, of everything.

"Well, the Imperial Chef gave me fresh fruit to thank me for saving his life," Hopper revealed. "Accepting fruit isn't against regulations."

The teammates sat down around the dining table and enjoyed the meal. They all missed having Commander Dragonfly among them.

Later, Radar filled a cup with stewed fruit. She left the lounging area to take it to the commander as she recovered. The rest of the team settled down to play cards and wait out their journey back to *Space Station Prime*.

✷ ✷ ✷

Hours later, Burrow yawned, stretched his spiked arms, and announced that he was tired of winning. His scorecard was full. That's when Scorpion asked Spoor to use the cards in a different way.

"Read my fortune," Scorpion requested.

Spoor gathered up the ordinary playing cards and handed them to Scorpion.

"You alone must shuffle the cards. By your hands will your fate be revealed," Spoor recited from an old tradition. It was rooted in an ancient culture based on Hindu philosophy that she and Scorpion shared.

Scorpion shuffled the deck and then handed it to Spoor as Hopper and Burrow watched. Hopper's legs twitched nervously.

"The first three cards represent the near future," Spoor announced as she flicked the top card from the deck and placed it on the table. "It's the Prince of Trouble."

Burrow and Hopper looked at each other and shrugged.

"That looks like a Jack of Diamonds to me," Burrow observed.

"Not to me," Scorpion stated.

Spoor flipped another card onto the table.

"The King of Darkness," she revealed.

"Okay, that's a plain old King of Spades," Burrow scoffed, but now he did not sound at all convinced.

"Um, Burrow, I don't like the sound of 'trouble' and 'darkness,'" Hopper revealed as he nervously thumped his footpads on the floor.

Spoor turned over the third card.

"Ace of Disaster!" Spoor gasped.

Suddenly, the power failed and the ship lurched as it unexpectedly dropped out of hyperspace.

CHAPTER 2

Bug Team Alpha swiftly reacted to their ship's unplanned halt in midflight. The emergency backup lighting engaged.

Spoor, Scorpion, Hopper and Burrow ran out of the lounge and down the corridor towards the bridge. As they passed the sleeping quarters, they saw Lt Radar standing in the doorway of Commander Dragonfly's cabin.

"What happened?" Radar asked.

"Don't know yet," Spoor replied. "Stay with the commander."

The four teammates arrived on the ship's bridge. Spoor did not need her enhanced scenting abilities to immediately smell smoke. They all smelled it.

Then they saw the black curls of smoke rising from the ship's flight control panel. Hopper used a small fire suppression cylinder to put out the minor blaze. Spoor and Scorpion quickly sat down in the pilot's and co-pilot's seats.

"The autopilot is fried," Scorpion said as she checked the controls.

"How did that happen?" Burrow asked as he looked over her shoulder.

"I'm not sure. When the autopilot failed, the hyperdrive engines shut down," Scorpion replied. "It's an automatic safety measure on a vessel of this type."

"Well then let's fire the engines back up and get out of here," Hopper suggested. "We can fly this ship without autopilot."

Spoor worked the controls, flipping switches and pressing buttons, trying to restart the ship's hyperdrive engines. Nothing happened. She kept trying.

"Engines aren't engaging," Spoor announced. "Scorpion, check the plasma fuel levels. Do we have a leak?"

"Fuel levels are where they should be," Scorpion

reported. "Huh. That's odd. The hyperdrive field generator is offline."

"We can't travel through hyperspace without that," Hopper said. "How are we going to travel without a hyperspace field?"

"The generator's not supposed to shut down. Something must have interfered with its operation," Spoor said as she worked a series of controls to bring the generator back online. Here she had success. "I've restarted the field generator, but it's going to take a while to build up enough energy to form a hyperspace field. We're going to have to travel through normal space for a while."

"Let's hope it's the scenic route," Burrow quipped. "Where are we?"

Scorpion activated a three-dimensional hologram of the course they had been travelling. The 3-D sphere in front of them displayed a planetary system with 10 planets of various sizes orbiting two suns.

A blue dot represented the Bug Team's ship. It was not moving. Scorpion pointed to a blinking white dot at the centre of the solar system.

"The navigational chart shows we're above Gehenna Six in the Perdition system. That's the Perdition pulsar," Scorpion said.

"Wait a minute. A pulsar? I think I know what happened," Spoor said. "The pulsar must have emitted a rogue flare of neutron energy that hit our ship. The radiation could have easily knocked out both our hyperspace field and the generator."

"I think you're right," Burrow agreed. "A pulsar normally emits neutron energy from fixed points on its surface and at regular intervals like an old-fashioned lighthouse. That's why we use them as navigational aids. But a rogue burst could go anywhere."

"It looks like we know where this one went," Hopper muttered.

"We're in more trouble than a pulsar burst," Spoor mentioned.

The lieutenant activated a new layer on the three-dimensional planetary chart. The whole Perdition solar system glowed red.

"The chart indicates we're in an interplanetary war zone," Spoor said.

Then she read the information on the computer.

"Multiple species have been at war over the minerals and frozen gases found on Gehenna Six. It's a gas giant with an asteroid ring and at least 12 moons," Spoor said. "The record shows that the Coalition offered to mediate an agreement but was refused. It's been a lawless free-for-all ever since."

"Sounds like a lousy place to break down," Burrow commented. "Let's get out of here."

"I'll go and brief the commander and Radar about our situation," Hopper said.

But he didn't make it very far. As he started to bounce from the bridge, a proximity alarm sounded on the control panel. The holo-chart showed multiple dots converging on the Coalition ship from opposite directions. Hopper leaped back towards his teammates.

"Incoming," Scorpion warned.

She touched the dots on the hologram and an info tab popped up, identifying the approaching ships.

"The spacecraft signatures register as Equinosian, Lycan and Sebekian," Scorpion reported. "Whoa, there's even a Draco in there. That's a strange mix."

Moments later the ships opened fire on each other. The Bug Team's vessel was caught in the middle.

Streamers of blaster energy streaked around the Coalition ship. Spoor and Scorpion tried to use the normal-space engines to move their ship out of the blistering crossfire. They did not succeed. Multiple alarms sounded warnings on the control panel.

"We're hit!" Scorpion reported. "Multiple hull punctures detected. We're bleeding air. I'm initiating automatic self-sealing repairs."

"Attention, Equinosian, Lycan and Sebekian ships!" Spoor broadcast on a wide comm to the battling spacecraft. "This is the Earth Colonial Coalition diplomatic vessel, *Peacemaker*. We're caught in your crossfire. Break off! Break off!"

The ships made another pass at each other. They did not seem to notice the Coalition vessel. If they did, they did not care.

"Where are the weapon controls?" Burrow growled as he scanned the bridge consoles.

"It's a diplomatic yacht, not a fighter," Hopper reminded his teammates. "There aren't any offensive weapons, only minimal defensive ones."

"Where?!?" Burrow turned to Hopper and flared his arms angrily.

Hopper pointed to a small console control panel to the left of the pilot's chair. Burrow activated the console.

"These aren't weapons, they're low-energy zappers and rescue flares. How am I supposed to fight anything with this stuff?" Burrow complained as he reviewed the yacht's limited defences.

A tactical hologram displayed a sphere around the Coalition vessel. The dots that represented the combatants flitted like fireflies inside the sphere.

Burrow worked the console controls with his buglike arms to combine the limited power of the low-energy zappers with that of the rescue flares. Then he stabbed his finger into the hologram and touched the battling dots.

His action activated a burst of intense energy that streaked from the Coalition ship and hit the dots. The dots stopped moving.

"The ships are disabled. Good work, Burrow," Scorpion said.

"I'll go give a report to the commander and Radar," Hopper said as he bounced from the bridge.

"It's not over yet," Spoor warned.

A second wave of spacecraft converged on the Bug Team's ship.

"Things are going from bad to worse," Scorpion said. "It looks like the fortune-telling cards got it right."

CHAPTER 3

Commander Dragonfly woke up in a wonderful bed. The mattress was fluffy. The sheets were silky smooth and had a soothing scent. The pillows were soft. At first Dragonfly thought she was resting on a cloud. Then she was jarred to full awareness by the sound of blaster fire and alarms.

"We're under attack," Dragonfly realized as she climbed out of bed. The sharp pain of her wounded wings reminded her why she was in bed in the first place. Helpful hands lifted her onto her feet.

"We're caught in a crossfire," Lt Radar told Dragonfly as she assisted her commanding officer. "The ship dropped out of hyperspace into a war zone."

"A pulsar shut down our hyperspace field generator," Hopper added as he helped Radar with the commander. "We've only got normal-space engines."

"I've got to get to the bridge," Dragonfly said.

The commander's torso, back and shoulders were wrapped in stiff plasticast medical bandages that made her very top-heavy. She almost fell over just trying to stand up. Dragonfly was normally light on her feet and used her wings to keep her balance. She was feeling the opposite right now.

Radar and Hopper assisted the commander. She put one arm around each of them, and they quickly helped her walk out of her cabin, down the corridor and to the bridge.

"Report status," Dragonfly ordered as soon as she arrived.

Her voice was full of authority even though she was being held upright by two of her lieutenants.

"I can't get us out of this crossfire. There are too many wild dogfights going on," Spoor replied from the pilot's seat. "They're shooting at anything and everything."

"What about our weapons?" Dragonfly asked.

"We have minimal defensive capabilities," Burrow responded. "I got off one good shot, but I can't seem to repeat it."

"Communications?" Dragonfly asked.

"I tried to contact them but no response," Spoor replied.

Suddenly, the whole ship shuddered. New alarms sounded from the main control console.

The shrill sounds forced Lt Radar to curl her vibration-sensitive antennae tight against her forehead.

"Another hit. It's the engine room. We're losing plasma fuel," Scorpion reported.

"Spoor, Scorpion, get to the engine room and stop that leak," Dragonfly ordered as she moved to take the pilot's chair.

"I . . . I don't know anything about these plasma engines, Commander," Spoor said as she jumped up from the seat to make room for the injured Dragonfly.

The lieutenant looked worried for the first time anyone could remember.

"Learn fast or we're all dead," Dragonfly replied firmly.

As Spoor and Scorpion left the bridge, Dragonfly dropped stiffly into the pilot's chair. Radar sat down in the co-pilot's seat next to her.

"Burrow, transfer tactical display to my panel," Radar said.

Burrow switched the holo-sphere he had used earlier over to Radar's co-pilot's station. A moment later a new barrage of blaster fire began to hit the diplomatic vessel.

Dragonfly did not even have the chance to put her hands on the controls before even more new alarms sounded.

"Hull breaches," Radar reported. "Self-repairs are offline."

"Burrow. Hopper. Find those breaches and seal them!" Dragonfly instructed.

Hopper swiftly bounced off the bridge and Burrow followed him.

"Radar, turn off those alarms, please. I need to concentrate," Dragonfly said.

"Gladly," Radar replied as she flipped controls to switch off the alerts. Her cranial antennae unfurled as soon as the harsh sounds were silenced.

Dragonfly worked the flight controls of the Coalition diplomatic vessel.

"Engine response is sluggish," Dragonfly said. "Minimal manoeuverability."

The commander tried to get the *Peacemaker* out of the battle zone from the pilot's seat. Blaster fire from multiple combatants continued to explode around the ship.

"Spoor was right. We can't get out of this crossfire," she said. "There are too many ships involved. It's like we're in the middle of a bee swarm and the bees have blasters."

"Incoming!" Radar shouted as she saw a dot heading towards them on the holographic tactical display. "There's a ship coming right at us!"

Commander Dragonfly worked the helm controls and attempted to move her vessel out of the way. But the *Peacemaker* moved like a snail. She could not avoid a collision.

Everyone on board felt the impact as the combatant's spacecraft hit the *Peacemaker* and then deflected away. The blow set both ships spinning.

The sudden centrifugal motion slammed Burrow and Hopper face-first into the damaged hull they were trying to seal. Unfortunately, Hopper was between Burrow and the bulkhead at the moment of impact. Hopper was flattened underneath his bulky, muscular teammate.

In the engine room, Spoor and Scorpion clasped their hands together to steady each other as they slid across the deck. Scorpion reached out and hooked one of her elbows around a supply pipe. As they came to a halt, Spoor grinned and offered up a high five.

And then the ship's artificial gravity failed. As the pair began to float weightlessly, a stray playing card drifted past them. It was the one Spoor had called the Ace of Disaster.

Back on the bridge, Dragonfly and Radar deployed emergency harnesses to hold them in their seats in the weightless conditions.

"The good news is we got knocked out of the 'bee swarm.' The bad news is we're caught in the gravity field of Gehenna Six," Dragonfly said. "It looks like we're heading for an uninitiated descent."

"What you mean is, we're going to crash," Radar interpreted.

"Yeah, we're going to crash," Dragonfly confirmed.

As Radar relayed this information to her teammates over the ship's internal comm, Commander Dragonfly did something she hated to do. Call for help.

"Calling *Space Station Prime*. Mayday. Mayday. Mayday. This is the Coalition diplomatic vessel *Peacemaker*," Dragonfly sent out over a dedicated comm link to the Bug Team's home base. "This is Commander Dragonfly to General Barrett. We have an uninitiated descent above Gehenna Six in the Perdition star system. Transmitting coordinates now. Mayday. Mayday. Mayday."

In the co-pilot's chair, Lt Radar magnified the holo-chart to zoom in on the asteroid rings and moons of the gas giant, Gehenna Six.

"We don't have many options for landing safely," Radar reported. Then she pointed to a dot. "Wait. That's the ship that hit us. It's heading for that moon inside the asteroid rings."

"I'm going to follow it," Dragonfly decided. "Whoever's in that ship might be a hostile, but they know this planetary system and probably know the safest place to land."

"Unless they're crashing just like us," Radar observed.

"We're about to find out," Dragonfly replied.

The commander used what little manoeuvering power was left in the flight controls and engines to nudge her spinning ship towards the large moon orbiting within the rings of Gehenna Six. The computer database showed that it was the size of a small planet and had enough gravity to hold an atmosphere. That was the only information available to Commander Dragonfly before she was forced to take her ship down.

CHAPTER 4

The *Peacemaker* was still spinning when it entered the moon's upper atmosphere. The Coalition vessel did not have a very aerodynamic design. Although it had small, stubby wings, the ship did not depend on the basic interactions of lift and drag. Antigravity fields had replaced re-entry aerodynamics a long time ago.

The *Peacemaker's* re-entry systems were not working anyway. Commander Dragonfly's piloting skills were put to the test.

"I've got to stop this spin and straighten us out," Dragonfly said as she blew open several of the service hatches in the cargo hold.

Air spewed out and acted like old-fashioned retro-rockets. Even though the thrust was minor, it helped stop the spin.

"We're still coming in too steep," Radar reported from the co-pilot's seat. "Hull temperature is rising."

Dragonfly had the DNA-enhanced wings of her namesake insect. She knew how to propel her body through the air both by instinct and from intensive training. Now she used that knowledge to try to fly a vessel that was about as manoeuverable as a falling brick.

The friction of the atmosphere started to heat up the hull of the *Peacemaker*. The ship was now in danger of becoming a molten falling brick.

"Initiating switchback manoeuver," Dragonfly said as she banked the vessel sharply.

The commander manoeuvered the ship in a back-and-forth path as if driving a truck down a steep, twisting mountain road.

The *Peacemaker*'s descent slowed to a manageable speed. Then the moon's gravity started to make its presence known.

CRAAAASH!

The sound of formerly floating dinner plates dropping to the deck in the dining area reached their ears. Dragonfly felt the heaviness of her plasticast bandages again.

"Automated landing systems are still offline. No re-entry antigrav, no stabilizers," Radar informed Dragonfly. "How are we going to put this bird on the ground?"

"Hard," Dragonfly replied grimly. "Where's the craft we were following? Did it land?"

"I'm calculating its flight path," Radar replied. She shook her head. "Its identifying signature is gone."

"It was probably already wrecked and dead when it hit us. I followed a ghost," Dragonfly muttered irritably.

"Commander! We've got a problem!" the voice of Lt Scorpion came over the ship's internal comm.

"Report," Dragonfly responded.

"There's a major hull breach in the engine room. The plasma fuel has been ignited. We're on fire," Scorpion said.

Suddenly, Dragonfly wondered if the *Peacemaker* would blow up before it even reached the ground.

"Hopper. Burrow. Assist Scorpion and Spoor in the engine room," Dragonfly ordered over the comm.

"On the way!" the two teammates replied as one.

"Put out that fire," Dragonfly said as calmly as she could.

Whatever was happening in the engine section, Dragonfly still had to concentrate on safely landing the ship. She guided the *Peacemaker* down through the moon's atmosphere, gliding back and forth in wide S-curves.

The descent took the ship through a system of massive thunderstorm clouds. The turbulence rattled the vessel down to its metal ribs.

"I can only make a few more turns and then we hit the dirt," Dragonfly calculated. She opened the internal comm to warn her team. "Bug Team Alpha, brace for impact!"

In the engine room, Burrow shielded Hopper with his body. He used his arm and leg spikes to staple them both to a bulkhead wall.

Spoor and Scorpion squirmed between a run of vertical supply pipes. It was like a cage and was the tightest space they could find.

On the bridge Commander Dragonfly activated the ship's landing sensors. The power blinked on and off, but a holographic image of the terrain ahead was displayed. The landscape looked mostly barren but very rocky.

Dragonfly aimed the *Peacemaker* as best she could towards the flattest stretch of ground she could see. Gravity, momentum and angle of descent did the rest.

The Coalition vessel hit the moon's surface belly-first and skidded. The ship remained intact long enough for the emergency crash foam to deploy on the bridge. Dragonfly and Radar were encased in protective cocoons.

A few moments later, all the little hull breaches caused by the space battle tore apart. The largest hole was in the engine section. It ripped apart like paper.

The entire rear of the ship separated and fell away, taking Spoor and Scorpion with it. Burrow and Hopper saw it go as they clung to the bulkhead that stayed with the ship.

Unfortunately, the section with the burning plasma fuel leak stayed as well. Flaming plasma spilled out behind the ship in a ribbon of fire.

Suddenly, the *Peacemaker* went airborne. The terrain was even rockier than Dragonfly had thought. The ship skidded up a small rise and was launched a few metres into the air.

When *Peacemaker* came down, the impact broke up the vessel into scrap. The bridge and sleeping sections tumbled end-over-end across the terrain. The plasma engines finally blew up.

Burrow and Hopper held onto their small piece of bulkhead as the blast sent them flying. When they hit the ground, they rolled across the landscape and eventually came to rest amid other debris from the wrecked ship.

Red desert sand blew over the shattered remains of the *Peacemaker*. A strong, steady breeze started to bury its carcass as the smoke and flames from the plasma fuel still poured out.

Commander Dragonfly slowly groaned back to consciousness. She was covered in . . . a cloud? Something white and fluffy surrounded her.

"Crash foam," Dragonfly remembered.

Dragonfly knew she was safe. She knew she could dig out of the foam. It was designed to dissolve at a touch after it had been activated. But she didn't have the strength to move. She had used all of her energy trying to save the ship and her team. Now she needed to restore that energy to heal. Commander Dragonfly drifted away from consciousness.

In the seat next to the commander, Lt Radar deactivated the crash foam and scraped it away. She gasped for fresh air. Instead she got a lung full of red dust.

When she looked around to get her bearings, the first thing Radar saw was the entire bridge section open to the air. The hull had been split as if Hopper had cracked it like an egg for an omelette. The next thing she noticed was the foam cocoon still surrounding Commander Dragonfly.

Radar reached out and touched the surface of the commander's crash foam cocoon. It dissolved to reveal Dragonfly as motionless as a corpse.

Alarmed, Radar used her sensitive antennae to detect any vibrations of a heartbeat. There was a steady

thump. Relieved, Lt Radar unstrapped her seat harness and stood up to help her commanding officer.

Radar's relief turned to shock when she looked behind her and saw that the bridge was the only part of the *Peacemaker* that remained.

A rocky red desert stretched out as far as the lieutenant could see. Waves of sand dunes rose up and down in the distance. The rest of the ship was missing. So was the rest of Bug Team Alpha.

CHAPTER 5

Lt Hopper slowly opened his eyes. All he saw was a bulkhead in front of his face. Every DNA-enhanced muscle in his body hurt. His long grasshopper legs were bent up against his chest in an unnatural position. He could barely breathe. Something was pressing him up against the bulkhead. Then Hopper realized it was Burrow.

"Burrow, buddy, are you okay?" Hopper rasped.

He tried to nudge his teammate with an elbow or a knee. There was no response. Burrow had spiked his arms and legs into the wall to protect Hopper, but now Hopper could not get out from under Burrow's protective embrace. Weak, Hopper fell unconscious again.

Then a steady breeze blew red sand up against the wreckage. It sifted through the cage of Burrow's arms and started to bury the teammates.

✳   ✳   ✳

As he slept, Burrow dreamed that he was sleeping on a lumpy bed. It wasn't very comfortable, so he woke up. That's when he realized it wasn't the bed in his dream that was lumpy. It was Lt Hopper.

Burrow pulled his arms out of the bulkhead and pushed away. Hopper fell out from under Burrow and tumbled down the small sand dune that the wind had formed.

"Hopper! Buddy, are you okay?" Burrow worried as he stumbled down the slope after his teammate.

"Maybe," Hopper replied groggily at the bottom of the dune. Then he felt a terrible pain in one of his grasshopper legs. "Or . . . maybe not."

Burrow took one look at Hopper's leg and knew the injury was serious. So did Hopper.

"I'll get you all fixed up in no time. Now, where did I put that medical kit?" Burrow tried to joke as he looked around. All Lt Burrow could see was scattered wreckage and red sand twisting in the wind.

"Commander Dragonfly has it. See?" Hopper said as he pointed towards a figure waving at him from a distant sand dune.

Burrow turned in the direction Hopper pointed, but he didn't see Commander Dragonfly. All he saw was a black, billowing smoke plume rising into the sky. When he looked back at Hopper, his teammate had fainted.

Lt Spoor woke up to find she was hanging at an odd angle in a tangled ball of supply pipes that had once been a part of the engine room. She managed to squirm her way out between the gaps and dropped onto the sand.

Scorpion was nowhere to be seen. Spoor knew she was lucky to be alive and unharmed. But she worried about the rest of her team. She desperately wanted to make sure they survived the crash.

A gust of wind blew a scrap of something up against her foot. Spoor reached down and picked it up. It was one of the playing cards. The six of hearts.

"Hearts means a friendship card. And number six represents the six members of the team. This is a good sign. It means I might find my friends," Spoor interpreted.

Lt Spoor was encouraged by the card. She turned around in a 360-degree circle, trying to decide in which direction to start looking for her teammates. Then she saw the black plume of smoke rising from the wreckage. She realized the playing card could also have a darker interpretation.

"I might find my teammates, but I might find them dead," Spoor muttered.

Lt Spoor tucked the card into a pocket of her clothing. Then she starting walking towards the smoke. She trudged across a bleak desert landscape of red sand and rocks.

There were small rises and dunes that led down into shallow depressions. The sky was rusty with iron oxide dust kicked up from the surface. A dull blue sun struggled to shed its light through the haze. The massive curve of the gas giant, Gehenna Six, arched across the horizon.

Except for the blue sun, Spoor thought the place looked a lot like the surface of Mars. The Bug Team used the Mars terrain for training inside the holographic battle simulator on *Space Station Prime*. But this was neither a holo-sim nor Mars. Spoor knew she was on a moon orbiting inside the rings of a planet similar to Saturn.

Gehenna Six loomed on the horizon like a pale ghost as Spoor shuffled towards the wraithlike plume of black smoke.

Lt Scorpion stumbled across the dry, hostile terrain. She was dizzy. Her vision and mind still spun from the crash landing. Not that she remembered much of it. She had no idea how she had survived.

Scorpion did not have a clear sense of direction, but any direction was okay with her as long as she kept moving. In her confusion, Scorpion wandered away from the crash site and into the desert. She didn't notice the black plume of smoke that was guiding the rest of her teammates.

Lt Spoor noticed a lone figure walking in the distance. The outline was blurry, almost like a mirage. She wasn't sure if what she saw was real. Her eyes could be deceived but her DNA-enhanced sense of smell could not.

Spoor opened up her nasal flaps to test for scents. Immediately she began sneezing. And sneezing. And sneezing from all the dust and sand in the air. She fought through the irritation until she managed to catch a trace of a very distinctive smell. It had the sharp tang of venom.

"Scorpion!" Spoor realized and started walking towards the figure.

When she reached her teammate, Spoor was glad to see her friend but was dismayed to see how dazed and confused she was.

"How many fingers am I holding up?" Spoor asked as she put two fingers in front of Scorpion's face.

"Ummm, five?" Scorpion guessed hopefully.

"You've got a concussion," Spoor diagnosed. "Well, it could be worse. We could be stranded on a moon in a declared war zone. Oh wait. We are."

Spoor turned Scorpion around and the two teammates walked slowly together towards the smoke plume.

Several minutes later Spoor and Scorpion reached the source of the smoke. They saw the smoke was coming from the smouldering remains of the hyperdrive engine. It rested in the middle of a giant skid mark that stretched across the desert terrain.

Spoor and Scorpion were also relieved to see Burrow shuffling towards them, carrying Hopper in his arms. Hopper was awake again and his leg was in a makeshift splint. The four teammates met at the smoke plume and were grateful that they had survived.

"But where are Commander Dragonfly and Radar?" Spoor wanted to know.

"We follow the skid and find out," Burrow replied grimly. "If they stayed with the bridge, that's where this probably leads."

The four teammates started walking along the scar in the ground. They turned their backs to the smoke plume, and did not notice it disappear like a mirage, as if it had never existed.

CHAPTER 6

Spoor, Scorpion, Burrow and Hopper found the wreckage of the bridge section about a half a kilometre away. They were all astonished at what they saw. The nose of the ship was intact. It rested in the sand at the end of the giant skid mark. The sleeping quarters had separated and come to a rest not far away. That's where the teammates saw Lt Radar. She stood in the doorway of an intact cabin and waved at them.

"You made it!" Spoor exclaimed.

"Where's the commander?" Burrow asked as he gently lowered Hopper onto his one good leg.

"Inside. She suffered more injuries in the crash. I set up a shelter as best I could," Radar replied.

"But I saw her near where Burrow and I landed," Hopper said.

"Impossible. Dragonfly has been unconscious since the crash," Radar replied.

"I'm sure I saw her," Hopper insisted.

He limped to the door of the cabin and peered inside. He saw Dragonfly asleep on the bed. There was a ghostly figure standing over her.

"What in the world!" Hopper exclaimed.

The figure dissolved like a wisp of smoke. Hopper's teammates rushed into the cabin but saw nothing.

"Either I'm dreaming while I'm awake or this place is haunted," Hopper shuddered.

"We're all hurt and exhausted," Radar declared. "We're stranded and we need to find food and water."

"We should look through the wreckage for any of the freeze-dried food packets that were on board," Burrow said.

Radar, Spoor, Scorpion and Burrow spread out from the camp to search for salvage. The injured Hopper stayed to keep watch over the commander. He sank down onto the floor of the cabin to rest his wounded leg and leaned his back up against the wall. He did not mean to fall asleep, but his body did not obey his good intentions.

Hopper drifted off into sleep. He immediately began to dream that he was 10 years old again, long before he had become Hopper. He was back on his family farm. He rode his pony as fast as he could through a field of tall grain. This wasn't a joyful gallop, however.

Black storm clouds boiled overhead. Lightning stabbed down from the sky. Thunder exploded. The wind whipped around him as if trying to grab him and smash him to the ground. He knew he was in terrible danger. He was terrified.

A tremendous clap of thunder jolted Hopper awake. The dream fell away, but the fear did not. Hopper limped to the door of the cabin and looked outside. A wall of storm clouds blackened the horizon, just like in his dream. Lightning flared in the distance. He could not see his teammates anywhere.

"This isn't good. They can't be caught out in that," Hopper muttered and fidgeted. If his leg had not been injured, he would have bounced as fast as he could to warn his teammates. Faster than his childhood pony.

Clouds of red sand started to swirl around the wreckage of the *Peacemaker*. Visibility dropped. Hopper worried how his teammates were going to find their way back to the shelter of the cabin. Suddenly, a blurry figure stumbled through the red haze. Then two. Then three. Burrow, Radar and Spoor rushed into the cabin.

"Where's Scorpion?" Hopper asked.

"She was right behind me a moment ago," Spoor said.

"I'll find her," Burrow declared and headed back out into the storm.

"This storm is dangerous," Hopper replied. "It reminds me of one from my childhood. It was bad."

"I think this is the same thunderstorm system we flew through on our way down," Radar realized. "It was a spine shaker."

"We can't leave the door open much longer. There's too much sand coming in the cabin. It could fill up," Spoor warned as the red stuff swirled around her ankles.

"We can't leave Burrow and Scorpion out there, either," Radar replied as she stood in the doorway and tried to use her antennae to search for their teammates. She pounded her fist on the wall in frustration. "I can't sense anything through all this interference."

"Wait! I see something!" Spoor shouted.

A shape trudged through the blinding sandstorm. It stopped just before it reached the cabin. It waved. Then two more shapes walked right through it as if it were a ghost and stumbled into the shelter.

Burrow and Scorpion fell to their knees and gasped for air. It took the combined strength of Radar, Spoor and Hopper to shut the door against the gale and secure it. The cabin was plunged into darkness.

"Um, did anyone salvage a light?" Hopper asked.

"It was on my list of things to do," Radar sighed.

The Bug Team hunkered down in the lightless cabin to wait out the storm. There was nothing else they could do. They were too tired to tell stories or jokes to keep their spirits up. One by one they gave in to their exhaustion and fell asleep.

✳   ✳   ✳

While in a deep doze, Burrow dreamed that he was on his first mission with Bug Team Alpha. He was plodding through a blizzard. He had lost sight of his teammates. Suddenly, he fell through thin ice into freezing water. Burrow tried to swim but was awkward with his new bug body. He flailed his arms and legs trying to keep afloat but failed. He started to sink. A moment later a pair of hands grabbed the shoulder pads of his combat armour. It was Lt Spoor. She was stretched out on her belly while Lt Scorpion held her ankles.

"I thought I smelled water, but it was just you, Burrow," Spoor laughed.

Burrow didn't know why she was laughing. This was serious.

They dragged him out of the hole in the ice, and he flopped onto his face. But instead of feeling ice against his skin, Burrow felt something gritty. That's when he woke up and realized his face was half-buried in a small drift of sand.

The cabin was still pitch black, but Burrow could hear that the storm had passed. It was quiet outside. He fumbled along the wall searching for the door. Along the way he stumbled over his teammates and woke them up. He found the latch and started to open the door.

"Burrow! Stop!" Radar suddenly warned as her antennae twitched.

CHAPTER 7

"Don't open that!" Radar exclaimed.

Her cranial antennae sensed the vibration of something big and dense outside of the cabin. But her warning came too late. Burrow had already opened the door before Radar's words came out.

"Look out!" Radar shouted.

A huge pile of sand flowed into the cabin. A giant drift had blown up against the side of the wreckage.

Burrow was caught in the avalanche. He churned his DNA-enhanced arms and legs just like in the water in his dream, but this time he was more skilled. The lieutenant easily dug his way free from the torrent of sand.

Burrow then used his strong and fast-moving bug arms to clear the drift away from the entrance.

The Bug Team emerged from the cabin to find a new landscape. The terrain had been scoured by the fierce winds. The skid mark was erased. The bridge was almost completely buried in the sand. The smaller pieces of wreckage had disappeared. Everything had either blown away or been buried, including any possible salvage.

Nonetheless, the air was clear. It revealed a bright blue sun, one of the two binary stars in the Perdition solar system. The pulsar that had disabled the *Peacemaker*'s engines was just a pinprick of light in the sky. The giant curve of the planet Gehenna Six dominated the horizon.

"At least all that dust and haze is gone. I can breathe again," Spoor commented as she opened her nasal flaps and took a long, slow inhale.

"Ahhhhh."

Her action reminded Burrow of something in his dream: *I thought I smelled water but it was just you.*

"Spoor, can you smell water?" Burrow asked.

"Sure, but I don't think there's any around here," Spoor replied as she looked at their surroundings doubtfully. Then she reconsidered.

"Still, that's a good idea. I can try," she told her teammates.

As the rest of the team removed sand from their cabin shelter, Spoor walked in a wide circle around the crash site. She sniffed the air with the DNA-enhanced scenting filaments on her nose, detecting and analysing faint airborne particles. The storm had cleansed the air of dust and she was able to pick up a trace of something promising.

"I don't smell water, but I do get whiffs of rusting metal. It could be salvage," Spoor told the team when she returned.

"We should go look for it," Burrow said.

"We should look for food and water first. Rusting metal isn't going to help us," Radar argued.

"We can't eat rusting metal," Scorpion agreed. "Hopper might be a great cook, but he isn't that good."

"Should we split up into search parties?" Burrow wondered.

"Well, we can't just sit here and do nothing," Hopper observed as he sat on a sand drift.

"I'll tell you what we're going to do," Commander Dragonfly declared as she stood in the door of the cabin.

The commander held herself upright with both arms on the doorframe. Her legs looked as if they were about to give way from under her. The upper half of her body was still wrapped in plasticast from her previous injuries.

Lt Radar rushed to support her commanding officer, but Dragonfly shook her head firmly at Radar. No.

"Bug Team Alpha, assemble!" Dragonfly ordered.

The teammates fell into formation in front of their commanding officer. They might have been dressed in ripped and ruined civilian attire, but they were Special Ops to the bone.

"Spoor. Follow the scent. Burrow. Go with her," Dragonfly said. "Radar. Search for vibrations of *Peacemaker* salvage that the storm buried. Scorpion. Help her. Hopper . . ."

Dragonfly faltered. The whole team leaned forward, ready to assist. Dragonfly held up her head defiantly.

"Hopper. Help me get to the bridge," Dragonfly finished. "Dismissed!"

As the Bug Team deployed to their assignments, Commander Dragonfly let herself lean on Hopper's shoulder. Together they limped towards the remains of the bridge.

"What do you expect to find in there?" Hopper asked wearily. His steps dragged.

"Hope," Dragonfly replied. "There's an SOS beacon. I want to see if it's working. I sent a Mayday to Barrett, but I don't know if it got through. We're stranded for now, but I don't intend on staying here very much longer."

Encouraged, Hopper's steps bounced back.

Spoor and Burrow followed the scent of rusting metal in search of salvage. What they found was a graveyard of wrecked spacecraft. The ships were broken apart and charred by fire. All of them were in various stages of burial by sand dunes.

As Burrow and Spoor walked through the metal ribs of rusting hulls, they counted the number of different species the ships belonged to.

"Sebekian, Lycan, Draco, Equinosian," Burrow observed. "It matches who we saw fighting in space."

The teammates climbed through the wreckage searching for useful salvage. Then suddenly, Spoor perked up and sniffed the air. A look of surprise and excitement overcame her face.

"I smell water!" she announced.

"Where?" Burrow wanted to know.

Lt Spoor pointed towards the centre of the spaceship graveyard. She and Burrow scrambled through the twisted hulls until they arrived at the source of the scent. They found a large pit in the middle of the graveyard. It was lined with small blue crystals that looked like diamonds. The crystals sparkled in the daylight.

"That doesn't look like water," Burrow commented.

"It sure smells like it," Spoor insisted. "Well, not exactly fresh water. It actually smells sort of sour."

Curious, Spoor knelt on the rim of the pit and reached for one of the crystals.

"Whoa!" Spoor exclaimed as the edge gave way. She started to slide down into the hollow.

Burrow reached out for her, but he started to slip down the slope right behind his teammate. He churned his arms and legs. It was just like in his dream. But this time Burrow rescued Spoor. He grabbed her by the wrist and crawled up the incline.

Their activity disturbed something living in the bottom of the pit. The crystals rippled and moved as multiple giant eyes emerged and opened their lids. The eyes swivelled for a moment before focusing on Burrow and Spoor.

Several octopuslike tentacles emerged from under the ground. They slid up the side of the pit towards the teammates. Spoor could smell the tentacles before she ever saw them. She looked over her shoulder and gasped.

"Burrow! Go, go, go!" Spoor shouted.

Burrow heard her alarm and glanced backwards. He saw the eyes. Then he felt a tentacle touch his leg.

"I'm going! I'm going!" Burrow replied.

Lt Burrow spiked through the sand and loose crystals with his bug arms and legs. The surface was not very stable. But as soon as he got close to the lip of the pit, he tossed Spoor up over the edge. Then Burrow used all of his limbs to propel himself out.

The two teammates ran to a safe distance away from the hole. The tentacles waved around in the air, looking for their prey, but then withdrew back where they came from.

CHAPTER 8

"What. Was. That?" Burrow asked breathlessly, not really expecting an answer.

"Pee!" Spoor said as she tried to spit something out of her mouth.

The lieutenants's whole face was wrinkled up in a grimace as she desperately tried to scrape the blue crystals off her face and lips. Her whole body was covered with the stuff.

A moment later Burrow understood. His face and body were also covered with crystals from the pit. Some fell into his mouth. The crystals dissolved on his tongue and suddenly he tasted what Spoor had tasted.

"Pee!" Burrow exclaimed.

"Yuck! Those crystals are that thing's dried waste. I didn't smell sour water. I smelled urine!" Spoor moaned.

The teammates sat down in the shade of a rusting spaceship strut and wiped their mouths.

"Well, this might not be a total loss," Burrow suggested. "We could rehydrate the crystals and purify the creature's urine in a makeshift solar condensation coil. We've got plenty of solar here and lots of salvage to construct a purification coil."

"That's a good idea, but how do we rehydrate the crystals? With our own pee?" Spoor replied. "And how do we know that Scorpion's pee isn't venomous?"

"Ha!" Burrow laughed despite himself. "I guess it can't be any worse than that pit monster's."

"I'm going to rest for a minute," Spoor sighed wearily. "Don't let me fall asleep."

"Okay," Burrow agreed as he yawned.

✱   ✱   ✱

Lt Spoor drifted into a deep slumber. She soon started to dream. She sat at the dining table aboard the *Peacemaker* and interpreted the fortune-telling cards for her friends. Someone Spoor didn't know walked up to the table. It was a female with equine features. A horse's head. Equinosian. The female placed an object on the table as if it was a card to be interpreted. It wasn't a card. It was a small square picture frame.

"Do you want me to interpret this?" Spoor asked.

"No, I want you to find this," the female replied.

Spoor picked up the frame. Inside she saw the image of the two of hearts.

"The two of hearts is a love card," Spoor said in the dream.

Then the image inside the frame changed from a two of hearts to a holo-pic of the Equinosian female and a child.

"Find me," the female urged as she disappeared like a wisp of smoke.

✳ ✳ ✳

Spoor awoke with a gasp. Burrow was snoring in the shade next to her.

"You let me fall asleep!" Spoor shouted at her teammate as she smacked him on the arm.

"Wha . . . what?" Burrow snorted awake.

"You let me fall asleep!" Spoor repeated. "Thank you!"

"Okay. You're welcome. Why?" Burrow mumbled groggily.

"I had a dream," Spoor replied.

"So?" Burrow said.

"In my Hindu culture, dreams have meaning. They're messages," Spoor told him. "I just got a message."

"From whom?" Burrow asked.

Spoor hesitated before answering. She wasn't sure that her teammate would believe her.

"A ghost," Spoor replied as she got to her feet and stood in the shadows of the spaceship graveyard.

"Hopper was right about this moon being haunted," Burrow shuddered. "We're in the middle of a graveyard. Who knows how many dead there are right under our feet. Let's just collect whatever salvage we can and get back to camp."

The teammates searched the remains of the wrecked ships and gathered items they could use for a solar condensation and purification system. They were not exactly sure how they were going to collect the pit monster's crystals, but decided to worry about that later. They also found several dried-up, mummified corpses, still strapped in their pilot seats. These they did not touch.

All the while, Spoor also searched for a small holo-pic frame.

At last the teammates headed back to camp. Spoor was disappointed that she had not found the holo-pic frame she had seen in her dream. She knew it had to be important. Spoor closed her eyes as she walked and tried to visualize the object in her mind.

"Where are you?" the lieutenant asked silently.

With her eyes closed, Spoor drifted away from Burrow and towards a small sand dune.

"Spoor!" Burrow shouted when he noticed she was heading off course.

Spoor opened her eyes to see she was standing in front of the dune. Something shiny attracted her attention. It glinted in the sun, half buried in the red sand.

"There you are!" Spoor exclaimed.

She dropped her armload of salvage to reach down and lift a small holo-pic frame from the sand dune. There wasn't an image in the frame anymore, but Spoor recognized the frame from her dream.

As soon as Spoor removed the frame from the dune, the sand shifted and fell away to reveal the hull of a spacecraft. Only a portion of the whole vessel was exposed, but there was no sign of damage.

"Burrow! Get over here!" Spoor shouted and waved at her teammate.

Lt Spoor started digging into the dune with her bare hands. When Burrow arrived, he added his DNA-enhanced digger arms to the effort.

A short time later, they had excavated a small spacecraft from the sand dune. They also found the bones of an Equinosian lying nearby. Spoor knew it had to be the pilot. As Burrow entered the ship to explore, Spoor reburied the pilot's remains nearby.

"I think this belongs to you," Spoor murmured as she placed the holo-pic frame with the bones.

"This ship is intact!" Burrow shouted excitedly from inside the spacecraft. "We can use it to get out of here!"

"Thank you," Spoor whispered to the grave.

When Spoor joined Burrow in the spacecraft, she saw that it was space worthy. It could fly. She sat in the pilot's seat with a little shiver. She had just buried the bones of the previous occupant.

Spoor switched on the ship's systems one by one. She was happy to discover that the power reserves had not failed. She didn't know how long the ship had been buried. The batteries could have died over time. As soon as the power came on, a holo-image appeared above the control panel. It showed an Equinosian female.

"I'm so sorry, son, I can't find him," the female said sadly. "I know I promised to bring back your dad, but I can't even locate his ship. There are so many wrecks . . ."

"Now we know why this ship is intact," Spoor realized. "It didn't crash, it came here on a rescue mission."

"I'm coming back home, son," the Equinosian promised. The holo-image switched off.

"She must have died right after that last entry and then a storm buried her ship," Burrow said. "She never made it."

"No, but we will, thanks to her," Spoor replied as she powered up the engines.

CHAPTER 9

Spoor and Burrow were filled with hope as the ship's engines came online with a roar. Then suddenly, their hope turned to concern. The whole vessel shuddered violently as the drive pods tried to blow sand from their exhaust ports. Indicator lights on the control panel blinked red. The engines shut down automatically with a slow wheeze.

"Ughhhhh," Burrow groaned in frustration.

"It's okay. It's okay," Spoor assured him. "The engines appear to still be intact. I think they just need to recharge."

"How long will that take?" Burrow asked.

"About two Earth Standard Hours," Spoor replied as she tapped a timer on the control panel that was counting down. "You go back to camp and tell the rest of the team about this ship. I'll stay here."

"Okay. Stay safe," Burrow said as he exited the cockpit.

"I will. I have a guardian ghost," Spoor smiled.

Burrow returned to the *Peacemaker* camp full of enthusiasm. He found Lt Hopper cooking food over a primitive campfire made from flammable debris gathered from their decimated space vessel.

Lt Radar's skills with her cranial antennae had reaped rewards. She and Scorpion had located packets of freeze-dried food from the crash site.

Hopper was preparing what he generously called "pan-seared stew." The "pan" was a flat slab of metal from the *Peacemaker*'s hull. The "stew" was the contents of some of the freeze-dried food packets all dumped together. There was no liquid to create a broth for an actual stew, so Hopper had to make do with what was available.

"I can't promise gourmet meals, but we'll survive," Hopper grinned.

"It doesn't have to be fancy, Hopper. It's going to be our last meal here!" Burrow declared.

"Last meal? We are not giving up, Burrow," Radar protested.

"Not on my watch," Commander Dragonfly agreed as she emerged from the shelter of the wrecked sleeping quarters.

The commander's torso and wings were still wrapped in bandages. She was physically weak, but her determination was stronger than ever.

The SOS beacon on the *Peacemaker*'s bridge had turned out to be dead. Commander Dragonfly, nevertheless, was resolved to save her team by whatever means possible.

"What I meant to say is that this might be our last meal here because Spoor and I found an intact ship. It still works, but Spoor is waiting for the engines to recharge," Burrow explained. "We can escape."

"What? Where?" his teammates exclaimed all at once.

"Spoor and I found a small Equinosian spacecraft buried in a sand dune," Burrow told Commander

Dragonfly and the rest of the Bug Team Alpha members. "I think she was guided to it in a dream that she had about –"

"I don't care how you found it. You said it was small. Can it get all of us off this moon?" Dragonfly asked.

"I'm . . . I'm not certain," Burrow admitted. "It is a single-pilot craft, and I'm not sure of its exact weight specs."

"Do you mean we might have to leave someone behind?" Hopper exclaimed.

He nearly dropped the freeze-dried food he was trying to cook.

"No one gets left behind," Commander Dragonfly declared. "Unless it's me."

The Bug Team members protested, but Dragonfly shut them down.

"I'm the one who has to decide. But I need all the available information before I do. Burrow, I want a full report," the commander said. "And Hopper, keep cooking. We're going to need our strength for whatever we have to do next."

Burrow gave his report to Commander Dragonfly as he gobbled down a portion of Lt Hopper's dry stew. When he was finished with both, Dragonfly dismissed him to take a portion of the meal to Spoor in the recharged ship.

As Burrow trotted out of the camp, the commander rallied the rest of the team. The sun was finally starting to set on the horizon. Night was approaching.

"We're moving to the Equinosian ship immediately. It's only a few kilometres from here," Dragonfly declared. "Hopper, you're responsible for the food packets. Radar, Scorpion, we need weapons. Burrow said that he and Spoor were attacked by a large, underground creature near the Equinosian ship. A pit monster."

In response, Scorpion gave the commander a double thumbs-up with her spiked venomous hands. Radar pulled a length of knife-sharp metal from the waistband of her clothing and swished it in front of her teammates. Scorpion and Radar exchanged confident glances.

"We're ready!" the teammates declared.

Hopper limped forward holding a small scrap of plastic sheeting like a bag.

"I've got the food!" he announced.

Commander Dragonfly picked up a handmade torch and lit it from the campfire. She glanced one last time at the ruined remains of the Coalition diplomatic yacht, *Peacemaker*.

"Move out," the commander said and led her team forwards.

The sky above the desert turned brilliant sunset colours as the sun sank below the horizon. The land was washed in deep red, then pink and then went dark.

The asteroids in the rings of Gehenna Six appeared on the horizon, illuminated by the giant gas planet. They peppered the sky like scattershot. Amid them floated the evidence of the solar system's ongoing war. Wreckage from hundreds of spacecraft twinkled like stars as the debris tumbled in low orbit around the desert moon.

"They're still fighting up there," Scorpion observed as she looked up at weapons fire visible in the night sky.

Blazing streaks of doomed combatants plunged down through the darkness like meteorites. Suddenly, some of the flaming debris hit the ground nearby and exploded like bombs.

"That was close!" Radar exclaimed as her antennae quivered with the concussive vibrations of the blast.

More streaks sizzled through the atmosphere and impacted even closer to the Bug Team. A chunk of burning hull rolled past the astonished teammates.

"We're in the crash zone," Commander Dragonfly realized. "Whatever ships are being shot in space are coming down here."

The commander handed Radar her torch and then ripped off her bandages, freeing her wounded wings.

"Get to the Equinosian ship, fast!" the commander ordered and pointed towards a pinprick of light in the distance that was coming from the cockpit of the resurrected vessel.

Scorpion and Radar supported Hopper between them as he half limped, half bounced as fast as he could.

Dragonfly buzzed above them and watched out for debris raining down around her team. She was so

concerned about what was above her in the sky that she did not notice what was happening on the ground. But Radar did. She felt it before she saw the danger rising up from below their feet.

"I'm getting vibes!" Radar warned her teammates just before the desert sands erupted with hordes of small, hungry night creatures.

CHAPTER 10

A giant swarm of bioluminescent animals emerged from the ground all around Bug Team Alpha. The creatures looked like small, six-legged, scuttling crabs with glowing hard shells.

The "crabs" instantly tried to eat each other. The Bug Team was caught in the middle of the chaos. Suddenly, the Bug Team became part of the meal as the creatures started to bite them.

"Burrow didn't say anything about this!" Scorpion shouted irritably as she pierced the creatures with her spikes and tossed them aside.

"Ow! Ow! Ow!" Hopper yelped as the creatures bit his DNA-enhanced feet and legs. He tried to jump and shake them off, but they gripped his skin with their tiny claws.

Radar used the flaming torch to singe the animals off Hopper. They dropped away from her teammate, but Radar could not protect herself from assault. The creatures swarmed her. Radar was forced to drop the torch in her desperate attempt to scrape the creatures off her body. The desert sand immediately snuffed the flame.

Bug Team Alpha was caught between two dangers. Fiery spaceship debris plummeted down on them from above. The carnivorous underground crab creatures swarmed up at them from below.

Suddenly, Burrow appeared, barrelling through the mass like a freight train. He used his bulk and DNA-enhanced strength to clear a path to his teammates. He picked up crab-covered Radar and Hopper, each one in a bug arm, and raced back towards the Equinosian ship.

Dragonfly buzzed down and grabbed Scorpion. The commander tried to lift Scorpion from harm, but her wings were still too weak. Dragonfly could not bear their combined weight. They never got off the ground.

"Commander! I can handle these pesky little creeps!" Scorpion insisted as she spiked and stomped on the creatures. "Get to the ship!"

"I'm the one who gives the orders around here, lieutenant," Dragonfly replied as she landed and picked up the dead torch. The commander used it like a mallet to smash the animals as they surrounded her and Scorpion.

Suddenly, a nearby area of sand began to sink like water flowing down a drain. Crab creatures over that spot fell with it.

Dragonfly and Scorpion almost joined them. They scrambled out of range as the sand slid into a newly formed pit. Tentacles reached up out of the hole and waved in the air. Then the tendrils reached out and scooped dozens of crab creatures into the pit. A huge mouth opened up and swallowed the crabs like pieces of popcorn.

"Burrow's pit monster!" Scorpion gasped.

"Or another one just like it!" Dragonfly realized. She snagged Scorpion by one of her wrists and half flew, half dragged her teammate away from the danger, no matter the cost to her wings.

One of the tentacles reached out to follow the fleeing teammates. Neither Dragonfly nor Scorpion knew how the monster tracked them – sound, scent or vibrations on the sand – but it managed to get them in its grip. The teammates were caught!

The tentacle tightened around its prey. Dragonfly's damaged wings were squeezed almost to the point of being crushed permanently. Scorpion's arms were pressed tight against her torso.

The teammates were lifted into the air and back towards the looming pit. Below their dangling feet, they saw multiple giant eyes blink up at them. The stupendous mouth started to open.

"Not today. Not ever," Scorpion gasped defiantly.

The lieutenant could not move her hands to stab the tentacle with her venomous spikes. Instead she used the next best thing – her teeth. Scorpion bit the pit monster!

There was no venom in Scorpion's bite, but she inflicted enough pain for the startled creature to relax its hold. Scorpion was suddenly able to move her hands just enough to twist her wrists and jam her spikes into the soft tentacle.

Scorpion's DNA-enhanced knockout venom instantly numbed the nerves of the tentacle. It quivered and flailed, and finally flopped to the ground just outside the pit. Dragonfly and Scorpion wriggled free of the grip. The monster paid no more attention to them as they staggered away and headed straight for the Equinosian ship.

The swarm of crab creatures had retreated back underground to escape the pit monster. Dragonfly and Scorpion had a clear path to the vessel. They clambered inside and secured the hatch. Spoor fired up the recharged engines.

The ship lifted off.

"I guess the weight specs are good for six occupants," Burrow observed as the single-pilot craft rose through the atmosphere.

"We are outta here!" Hopper cheered.

"We're not in the clear yet," Dragonfly said and pointed through the front window at the space battle raging ahead of them.

"I don't see any controls for a weapons system or shields," Burrow informed his teammates as he squeezed next to Spoor at the main control panel.

Suddenly, blaster fire came at them from above.

"Cease fire! Cease fire! We are a neutral vessel!" Dragonfly broadcast on a wide comm from the ship. "We are citizens of the Earth Colonial Coalition!"

"Commander Dragonfly! Is that you? Respond!" General Barrett's voice came back over the comm unexpectedly.

"General! Yes! We're in an Equinosian ship. I'm transmitting its identification signature now," Dragonfly replied.

A few moments later an energy field surrounded the little ship.

"I've extended our shields around you," Barrett said. "Activating magnetic grappling beams. We're bringing you aboard."

The nose of the Equinosian vessel turned around. That's when the Bug Team saw they were being pulled towards a Coalition battleship.

"I guess he heard my Mayday after all," Dragonfly said.

Barrett's battleship protected the Bug Team's borrowed ship until it was safely onboard. The general

met them in the landing bay as they stepped off the little ship. A medical team stood by.

"I give you an easy, diplomatic mission and this is what happens," Barrett joked. His humour hid the fact that he had been seriously worried about the team.

"Yes, sir. Combat missions are a lot safer," Dragonfly replied.

"Let's get you patched up first, and then I want a full report," Barrett said and waved over the medical team.

After one Earth Standard Week, Bug Team Alpha arrived on the planet Equinos. They had located the son of the pilot whose ship had saved their lives. It was important to them to let him know the fate of his mother and the significant role she had played in their survival. He was no longer the boy depicted in the holo-pic that Spoor had seen in her dream. He was now a young man. It turned out that the spacecraft had been buried for many years.

"We don't know why her ghost was so intent on helping us," Dragonfly said. "But she guided us to her ship and saved our lives."

"I think she wanted you to tell me what had happened to her," the son said. "My mother was a very determined person. It's why she went searching for my father in the first place."

"Then we have fulfilled her wish," Dragonfly said. "Mission accomplished."

Mission report

TO: GENERAL JAMES CLAUDIUS BARRETT, COMMANDER OF COLONIAL ARMED FORCES

FROM: COMMANDER ARIEL "DRAGONFLY" CARTER, BUG TEAM ALPHA

SUBJECT: AFTER ACTION REPORT

MISSION DETAILS:

Mission Planet: Unnamed moon
   in orbit around Gehenna Six
Mission Parameters: Uninitiated descent and landing
Mission Team: Bug Team Alpha [BTA]
* Commander Ariel "Dragonfly" Carter
* Lt Anushka "Spoor" Kumar
* Lt Akiko "Radar" Murasaki
* Lt Liu "Hopper" Yu
* Lt Gustav "Burrow" Von Braun
* Lt Madhuri "Scorpion" Singh

MISSION SUMMARY:

BTA departed Zohatepa for *Space Station Prime* aboard diplomatic vessel *Peacemaker*. Unexpected hyperdrive failure occurred in Perdition star system due to rogue neutron energy burst from the system's pulsar.

Area designated a war zone due to multi-species conflict over planetary resources within the system.

Peacemaker caught in crossfire of multiple privateer ships.

Defensive protocols initiated and exhausted. Mayday transmitted to *Space Station Prime*. *Peacemaker* forced into uninitiated descent and landing on moon orbiting Gehenna Six. *Peacemaker* destroyed in landing. BTA survival rate: 100 per cent.

Survival protocols initiated: food, water, shelter. While investigating salvage from a spacecraft "graveyard," hostile life form was encountered.

Unconventional experiences by several BTA members contributed information that led to the discovery of a buried, operational Equinosian spacecraft. BTA utilized the craft to escape the moon and intersect with Colonial Armed Forces battleship *Andromedis*.

APPENDIX 1: EQUIPMENT REQUISITION
Diplomatic space yacht *Peacemaker*
Unregistered Equinosian vessel [salvage]

APPENDIX 2: PARTICIPANTS:
Bug Team Alpha [mission participants listed above]

END REPORT

Glossary

aerodynamics ability of something to move easily and quickly through the air

asteroid chunk of rock too small to be called a planet that orbits a star

bioluminescent able to produce light as a living thing

DNA molecule that carries all of the instructions to make a living thing and keep it working; DNA is short for deoxyribonucleic acid

hologram three-dimensional picture formed by light beams from a laser or other light source

neutron particle in the nucleus of an atom that has no electric charge

plasma matter that is a collection of hot, charged atoms, such as those found in a fluorescent lightbulb, neon sign or star

pulsar neutron star that sends out radio waves, light and other kinds of energy

radiation rays of energy given off by certain elements

About the author

Laurie S Sutton has been interested in science fiction ever since she first saw the *Sputnik* satellite speed across the night sky as a very young child. By 12 years old, she was reading books by classic sci-fi authors Robert Heinlein, Isaac Azimov and Arthur C Clarke. Then she discovered *STAR TREK*.

Laurie's love of outer space has led her to write *STAR TREK* comics for *DC* Comics, *Malibu* Comics and *Marvel* Comics. From her home in Florida, USA, she has watched many Space Shuttle launches blaze a trail though the sky. Now she watches the night sky as the International Space Station sails overhead instead of *Sputnik*.

About the illustrator

James Nathaniel is a digital comic book artist and illustrator from the UK. With a graphics tablet and pen, he produces dramatic narrative focused fantasy, science fiction and non-fiction work. His work is the result of inspiration accumulated from the likes of Sean Gordon Murphy, Jake Wyatt, Jamie Hewlett and Jon Foster, as well as many years playing video games and watching films. In the near future, James hopes to write and illustrate his own graphic novels from stories he's been developing over the years.

Discussion questions

1. The Bug Team was in a transport ship that was not meant for combat. Would their fate have been different if they had been travelling this route in a combat ship? Why or why not?

2. How did Commander Dragonfly's injuries from the incident on planet Zohatepa hinder her ability to lead? In what ways did she still show leadership? How did the other Bug Team members step in to lead and work together?

3. Discuss the role that dreams played in the story. Why do you think the Bug Team members had so many dreams? How were the dreams helpful to their escape?

Writing prompts

1. Imagine you were a member of Bug Team Alpha. What bug or insect would you model your new body after? Using descriptive language, write about what physical features and elite fighting skills you would have.

2. Fortune telling, dreams and warnings all play an important role in this book. Write about a time you thought you might be receiving a warning or a sign about something. Did you listen? Write about what happened and what the outcome was.

3. What happens next in the story? You decide! Write the next chapter in this book. Does Bug Team Alpha go on to another mission? Do Commander Dragonfly's wings heal? What happens to the son of the ghost from the planet Equinos?

BUG TEAM ALPHA

BUG TEAM ALPHA

THE DIG

When an archaeologist goes missing and presumed kidnapped during an expedition, Bug Team Alpha is called in to help.

BUG TEAM ALPHA

THE DRACO

The president of Earth has been kidnapped by Draco warrior forces. Can Bug Team Alpha rescue her in time?

BUG TEAM ALPHA

INVISIBLE ENEMY

Talos is under attack, but no one can see exactly who - or what - the enemy is. Bug Team Alpha is called in to fight.

BUG TEAM ALPHA

STRANDED

What happens when Bug Team Alpha's transport ship crash lands after intersecting an interplanetary war zone? Read *Stranded* to find out!